For Talia, with love from Granny D.
And with thanks to Deborah Kilcollins,
who sparked this story
—D. H.

For Marianne, my wonderful oodle doodle
apple strudel mum
—S. M.

tiger tales
an imprint of ME Media, LLC
202 Old Ridgefield Road, Wilton, CT 06897
Published in the United States 2008
Originally published in Great Britain 2007
by Little Tiger Press
an imprint of Magi Publications
Text copyright © 2007 Diana Hendry
Illustrations copyright © 2007 Sarah Massini
CIP data is available
ISBN-13: 978-1-58925-075-8
ISBN-10: 1-58925-075-3
Printed in Singapore
All rights reserved
1 3 5 7 9 10 8 6 4 2

Oodles of Noodles Oodles of Noodles
Oodles of Noodles Oodles of Noodles Oodles of Noodles Oodles of Noodles
Oodles of Noodles Oodles of Noodles Oodles of Noodles Oodles of Noodles
Oodles of Noodles Oodles of Noodles

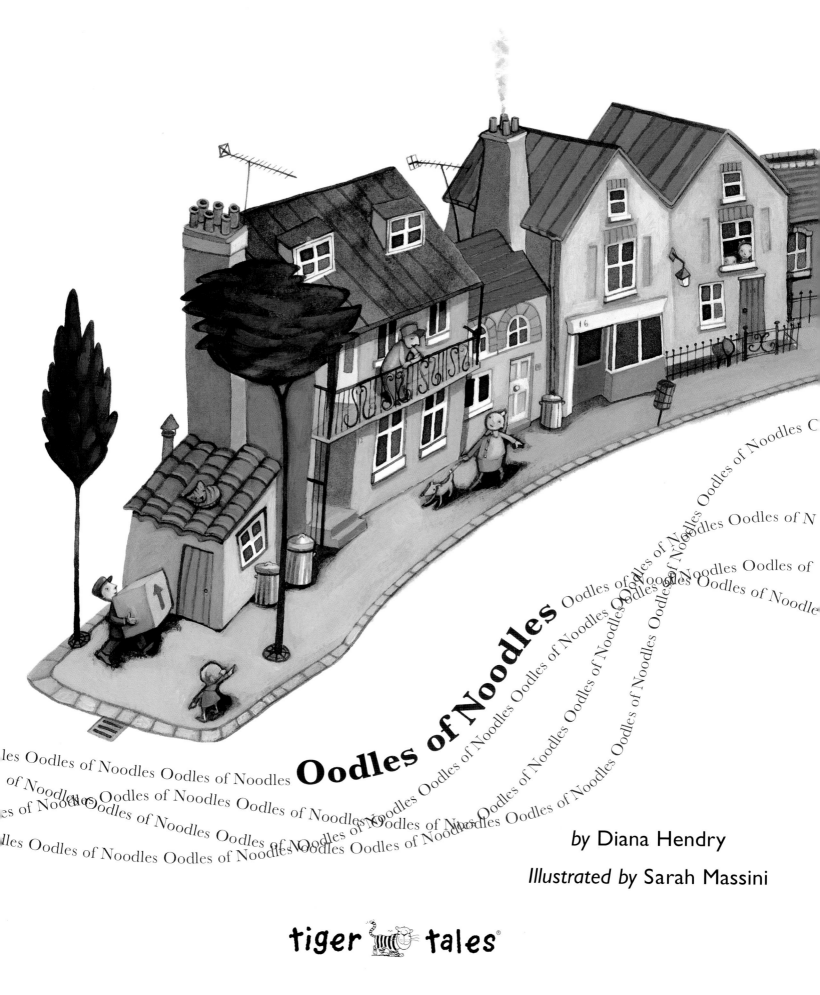

Oodles of Noodles

by Diana Hendry

Illustrated by Sarah Massini

tiger tales

On her birthday, Mrs. Mungo was given a **pasta-making machine**.

"*Noodles* for slurping, *noodles* for stew, *noodles* for me, and *noodles* for you!" sang Mrs. Mungo.

"I like **burgers**," said Ava.

"And **fries**," said Ben.

Mrs. Mungo put the **pasta maker** on the kitchen table, got a bowl, and made a **HUGE** ball of pasta dough.

"*Noodles* with garlic, *noodles* with *sauce!*" she sang.

"**Burgers** with ketchup," said Ava.

"And **fries**," said Ben.

As soon as Ava and Ben left for school, Mrs. Mungo began **rolling** out the pasta.

It was **HARD** work turning the handle of the machine and **rolling** the pasta thinner and thinner.

"It's worth it," said Mrs. Mungo. "I'll soon have

oodles of *noodles*."

And at that moment, something *very* **STRANGE** happened. The **pasta maker** began working all by itself. **Long, long loops** of *noodles* rolled out of the **machine**. Soon Mrs. Mungo was **tightly** tucked in a *noodle* sleeping bag.

At school, there were *noodles*, **onions**, and **peas** for lunch.

Ava and Ben ate
the **onions** and **peas**.

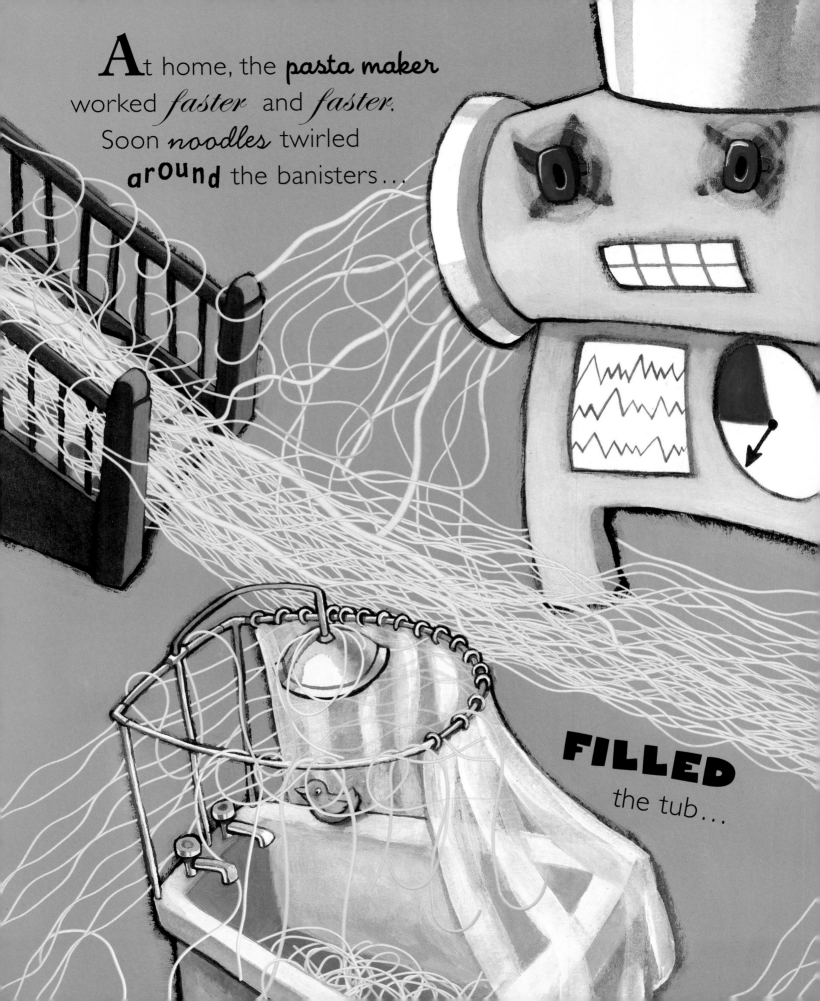

At home, the **pasta maker** worked *faster* and *faster*. Soon *noodles* twirled **around** the banisters…

FILLED the tub…

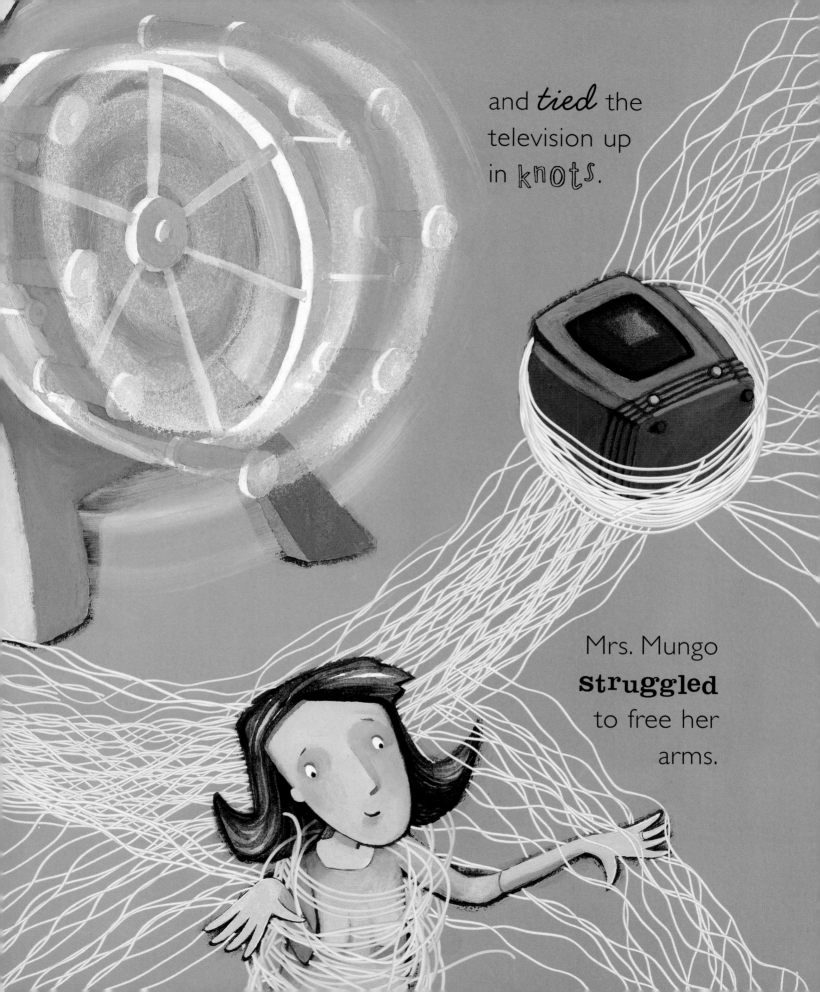

and *tied* the
television up
in *knots*.

Mrs. Mungo
struggled
to free her
arms.

"**STOP! STOP!**" Mrs. Mungo cried to the **pasta maker**.
But it didn't.
"There must be a magic word," thought Mrs. Mungo.
"*Doodle!*" she shouted. "*Poodle* and *doodle* and
apple strudel!"
But the **pasta maker** took
no notice.

Instead the *noodles* *slithered* under the door and **down** the sidewalk.

Outside *noodles* wound themselves
around gates, w**r**a**pp**ed **around** lampposts,
and d**a**n**gled** from trees.

Soon *everyone* in the street came out and began filling their saucepans with *noodles*.

The *noodles* ran down the road until they reached the school.

The children in the playground thought the *noodles* were *wonderful*. They made *noodle* jump ropes and *noodle* hula hoops—all except Ava and Ben.

"*Noodles!*" cried Ben.

"*Oodles* and *oodles* and *oodles* of *noodles!*" cried Ava.

"Quick, Ben! **HOME!** I think Mom needs us."

And as fast as they could, Ava and Ben ran.
It wasn't easy.

When at last they reached the kitchen, the **pasta maker** was still **WHIZZING** out noodles.

They kept tripping over *noodles* and **bumping** into *noodle* collectors.

All they could see of their mother was her head. She was *totally* **noodled**.

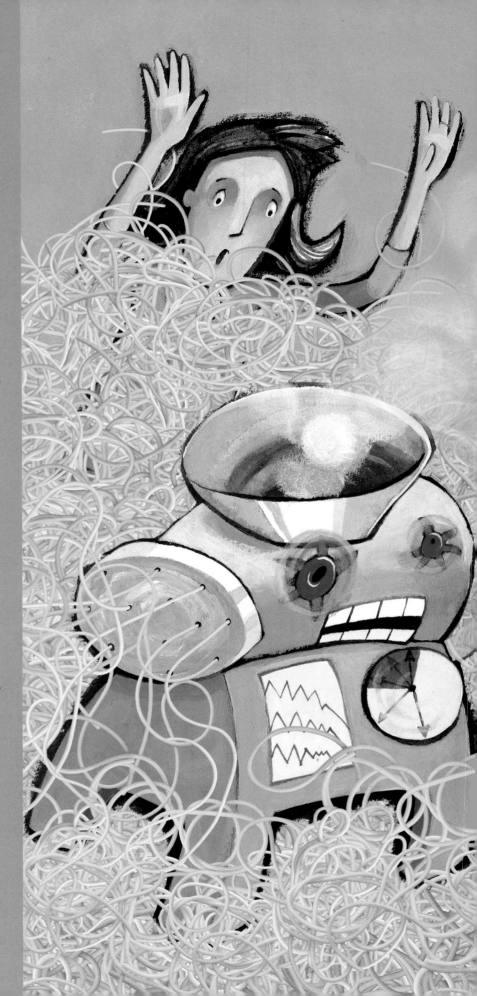

"**It won't stop!**" wept Mrs. Mungo. "All I said was '*oodles of noodles*' and it *noodled* and *noodled* and *noodled*. I've tried every magic word I know."

"Did you try saying it the other way around?" asked Ben.

"**I didn't think of that**," said his mother.

So all together and very loudly, they said, "*Noodles of oodles!*"

And with a groan of relief, the **pasta maker** stopped.

Ben and Ava unwrapped
their mother. She *flopped* in a
chair as Ava wound
the *noodles* into
a great big ball.